Helena Pielichaty (pronounced Pierre-li-hatty)
has written numerous books for children, including
Simone's Letters, which was nominated for the
Carnegie Medal, and the popular After School
Club series. A long-standing Huddersfield Town
supporter, there are few who could write with as
much enthusiasm about girls' football. A local
girls' under 11s team helps with the inspiration
and tactical know-how, but Helena has been
an avid fan of women's football for many years.
It clearly runs in the family: her aunt was in a
women's team in the 1950s and her daughter
has been playing since she was ten (she is now
twenty-six!). Helena lives in Nottinghamshire with
her husband and has two grown-up children.

The Girls FC series

Has Anyone Seen Our Striker?

Helena Pielichaty

WALKER
BOOKS

For Alice

First published 2011 by Walker Books Ltd
87 Vauxhall Walk, London SE11 5HJ

10 9 8 7 6 5 4 3 2 1

This book has been typeset in Helvetica and Handwriter

Printed and bound in Great Britain by Clays Ltd, St Ives plc

British Library Cataloguing in Publication Data:
a catalogue record for this book is available from the British Library

ISBN 978-1-4063-1731-2

www.walker.co.uk

☆ ☆ The Team ☆ ☆

- ☆ **Megan "Meggo" Fawcett** GOAL
- ☆ **Petra "Wardy" Ward** DEFENCE
- ☆ **Lucy "Goose" Skidmore** DEFENCE
- ☆ **Dylan "Dyl" or "Psycho 1" McNeil** LEFT WING
- ☆ **Holly "Hols" or "Wonder" Woolcock** DEFENCE
- ☆ **Veronika "Nika" Kozak** MIDFIELD
- ☆ **Jenny-Jane "JJ" or "Hoggy" Bayliss** MIDFIELD
- ☆ **Gemma "Hursty" Hurst** MIDFIELD
- ☆ **Eve "Akky" Akboh** STRIKER
- ☆ **Tabinda "Tabby" or "Tabs" Shah** STRIKER/MIDFIELD
- ☆ **Daisy "Dayz" or "Psycho 2" McNeil** RIGHT WING
- ☆ **Amy "Minto" or "Lil Posh" Minter** VARIOUS

Official name: Parrs Under 11s, also known as the Parsnips

Ground: Lornton FC, Low Road, Lornton

Capacity: 500

Affiliated to: the Nettie Honeyball Women's League
junior division

Sponsors: Sweet Peas Garden Centre, Mowborough

Club colours: red and white; red shirts with white sleeves,
white shorts, red socks with white trim

Coach: Hannah Preston

Assistant coach: Katie Regan

☆ ☆ Star Player ☆ ☆

☆ **Age:** 10

☆ **Birthday:** 22 August - which makes me the youngest in my class

☆ **School:** Mowborough Primary (but not for much longer - boo hoo!)

☆ **Position in team:** striker

☆ **Likes:** CHOCOLATE

☆ **Dislikes:** days without chocolate

☆ **Supports:** England, England Women, Arsenal Ladies

☆ **Favourite player(s) on team:** Gemma (has to be)

☆ **Best football moment:** scoring after a great cross from Gemma

☆ **Match preparation:** First thing I do is check the weather outside. Mum makes me have breakfast. That's about it.

Eve "Akky" Akboh

☆ **Have you got a lucky mascot or a ritual you have to do before or after a match?**
Not really, but if I score a goal during the match I always look up at the sky in case Dad's watching.

☆ **What do you do in your spare time?**
Spare time? What's that? Every week my mum gives me a list of chores as long as an octopus's arm. Then there's church on Sunday and after-school club mid-week. Playing football is what I do in my spare time, dude!

☆ **Favourite book(s):** Amazing Grace by Mary Hoffman. It's a picture book, but I looked just like Grace when I was little. Amazing Eve!

☆ **Favourite band(s):** Rihanna, The Black Eyed Peas, Tinie Tempah

☆ **Favourite film:** School of Rock

☆ **Favourite TV programme(s):** Are You Smarter Than a 10 Year Old?

Pre-match Interview

Yo, my name is Eve Akboh and I am a
striker for the Parrs football team.
I am going to tell you about the
end of the second season. I wish I
didn't have to because the end of
the second season also means the
end of my time as a Parr. It's an
Under 11s team and I'll be twelve
soon, so I won't be eligible to play
for them again.

I'm gutted. I'm really going
to miss being on the team, even
though Gemma, my favourite player,
has already left due to unforeseen
circumstances. Still, feeling sorry
for myself won't change anything.
And I should know. I've tried it
often enough!

Anyway, here are the remaining
fixtures:

Misslecott Goldstars (Nettie
Honeyball Cup quarter final)
Cuddlethorpe Tigers (away)
Grove Belles (away)
Southfields Athletic (home)
Cup weekend – Nettie Honeyball
Cup semifinal: Teams TBC
Lutton Ash Angels (home)

It's not a lot, is it? Four league
matches and a cup match. I suppose
if we win the quarter final we buy
ourselves an extra match (or two)
but it's still going to be torture
every time I cross a game off my
list. Oh well. I'd better get on
with it, I suppose.

Your friend, as always,
Eve xxx

Pre-match Interview Part 2

Sorry about this, but Megan says I need to explain what I mean about Gemma and the "unforeseen circumstances". That's because she has no feelings. I am writing this part superfast to get it over with. Here goes...

The unforeseen circumstances started when the Cuddlethorpe Tigers match was abandoned because of heavy snow. My mum would have picked me up but her car broke down on the motorway, so Gemma invited me back to her house to wait.

Being invited to Gemma's should have been the coolest thing since sliced gherkins, but I couldn't relax because I was worried about Mum and also Gemma was being weird with me. I didn't know why at the time but everything I said seemed to annoy her. Then, during lunch, I mentioned to her dad, Kriss, how brilliant she was at playing football and she went bananas! Yelling that she hated me and stuff like that. I couldn't believe it. I'd thought we were friends.

I apologized for upsetting her (even though I wasn't really sure what I'd done wrong) and she apologized too and went back to normal. Actually, she didn't go back to normal; it was better than that. For the first time ever she opened up to me. "Let me show you something," she said and got out these scrapbooks from when her dad played for West Ham. *The* West Ham. It turned out that Kriss had been a professional footballer when he was younger. He'd nearly played for England, but all the media attention from the paparazzi had been too much. Gemma said it had been terrifying being followed everywhere, so in the end he packed it in and they came to live in Mowborough.

I would never have guessed Gemma had a background like that, although I suppose her stupendous football skills had to come from somewhere. Anyway, after we'd finished looking at the scrapbooks, my mum phoned to say she was home and Kriss took me back and that was that.

Everything was better than ever between us, both on the team and at after-school club, until the day of the Greenbow match.

What happened was that my brothers, Samuel and Claude, turned up to watch along with their mates Marlon and Theo. I admit I had told them about Gemma's dad playing for West Ham. Maybe I shouldn't have, and after what happened next I really wished I hadn't, but I did. Anyway, they went to talk to him and after I'd been subbed I joined in.

It was pretty uneventful until Gemma and Amy arrived just after the second half had started. Gemma seemed uncomfortable with everyone crowding round. I was about to tell Claude to give her some space when Marlon asked if he could take a picture. I think he meant of Kriss, but Gemma looked horrified. I remembered then what she'd said about the paparazzi from when she was little – but it was too late. Marlon had already pressed the button. His camera flashed and Gemma bolted, her dad and Amy in hot pursuit.

I just stood there, rooted to the spot, staring after them until they disappeared.

And that's what happened. Gemma might tell you something different. Amy Minter might tell you something different. But that's what happened, I swear on my dad's grave.

1

It goes without saying the rest of that weekend was pretty rubbish. I tried phoning Gemma's house a couple of times but nobody was picking up. I was on tenterhooks waiting for after-school club on Monday, when I'd see Gemma, so I could apologize.

Only Gemma didn't show. Amy Minter came alone, and when I asked where Gemma was she put a hand in front of my face and said, "Don't speak to me!"

So I wrote "Where's G?" on a Post-it and stuck that in front of her nose. She scribbled back "What part of 'don't speak to me' don't you understand?"

And I thought, Fine, dude, be like that, and I went to help little Pawel and his brother stick lentils to stuff.

The same thing happened on Tuesday. No Gemma and a well grouchy Amy. By the time I arrived at Mowborough Sports Hall later that evening for training I didn't know what to expect.

The first clue I had that something odd was going to happen was when I walked in and saw Kriss talking to our coaches, Hannah and Katie. There was no sign of Gemma. I wanted to say hello to Kriss, but he looked so solemn it put me off.

The next clue was when Hannah asked us all to sit on the benches rather than warm up. I sat between Petra and Nika.

"OK, girls. This is Gemma's dad, Kriss. As you know, Gemma left the match early on Saturday. I told you at the time it was because she was poorly but there was a bit more to it than that..."

My heart did a double backflip. "A bit more to it" had to be about me. Was he going to tell everyone about me and my big mouth? I felt my skin prickle as Kriss began to talk. He started off by telling everyone about when he used to be a footballer and how the family had lived in London.

"What? You played for the Hammers?" Megan interrupted.

"Among others." Kriss smiled.

"Wow!"

"What position did you play?" Lucy asked.

"Centre-back."

The questions flew thick and fast until eventually Hannah stepped in. "Kriss isn't here to talk about his career," she informed us.

I glanced across at Amy. Her cold eyes told me all I needed to know about what he was here to talk about. I looked away and focused on the floor.

"Don't worry. Everything about me is on the Internet," Kriss told everyone, then added grimly, "And that's the problem. When you're in the public eye, everything you do is out there for anyone to read about. Everything. From boring stuff like what you have for breakfast to how much you earn a week. The lack of privacy can get on your nerves after a while. I tried to keep a low profile off the pitch and lead as normal a life as possible for my kids' sake, but I was away a lot and so was Gemma's mum because she was building up her kitchen business. It meant Gemma spent a lot of time with her nanny. What we didn't know was that the nanny was spending a lot of her time with some very dodgy characters…"

Up to that point Kriss hadn't said anything I didn't know but this was the first time I'd heard mention of a nanny. Kriss took a deep breath before continuing. "One day we came home to find that both Gemma and the nanny had disappeared. There was just a note, saying they'd both been kidnapped. It wasn't true. Only Gemma had been kidnapped. The nanny, whose boyfriend had planned the whole thing, had already gone on the run."

My mouth fell open in shock. Gemma definitely hadn't told me that! There were gasps and cries of "Poor Gemma" from around the benches.

"Was she hurt?" Petra asked.

Kriss shook his head. "She wasn't hurt. They didn't tie her up or anything like that and luckily the sleazeballs were caught soon afterwards. Things settled down until the trial a few months later. Then the nanny made up a lot of lies about us and the media went into overdrive, camping outside the house, banging on the car windows, asking if this was true and that was true. It was a horrendous time. Gemma never really got over it."

There was silence for a moment. "That nanny wants to rot in jail," JJ said.

I didn't know what to think. I felt numb.

"But why are you telling us all this now? Does Gemma want us to know?" Megan asked.

"Yes, she does," Kriss replied. "She hopes it will help you understand why she ran off on Saturday."

"Wasn't she ill?" Petra asked.

"No."

My stomach clenched. Here it comes, I thought.

"Someone recognized me and took a photograph while Gemma was standing next to me. It wouldn't have been so bad if the camera hadn't flashed in her eyes but it did and that triggered her bad memories."

"She was absolutely petrified," Amy added for good measure.

It was too much. Tears as big as daffodil bulbs began rolling down my cheeks. "I'm so sorry," I blurted and began babbling incoherently about Claude and Marlon and not knowing about nannies.

"What's she on about?" someone whispered. "Who's Marlon?"

But I couldn't answer. I was in full flow. Shoulders heaving; the works. Kriss dashed across, knelt right down in front of me and pushed a tissue into my hand. "Oh, Eve, sweetheart. Don't worry. It was just one of those things. Nobody's blaming you. Gemma certainly isn't."

I glanced up warily. "Isn't she?"

"No. Not a bit."

I felt better then. "Oh," I said and blew into the tissue. I made such a loud noise that everyone laughed. Kriss rubbed the top of my head and returned to his seat.

"If it helps, none of us will mention anything when we see her," Megan told him. "We won't, will we?" She looked round and all of us were nodding in agreement.

Kriss sighed and exchanged a look with Hannah.

"The thing is, you won't be seeing her. Gemma doesn't want to play football any more," Hannah announced.

"But she has to! We've got a cup match on Saturday…" Megan protested.

"I'm working on it," Kriss assured her. "I think it's important she plays, too, but she's convinced herself the media will start showing an interest."

Megan gawped at him. "Interest? In a girls' under elevens team? They don't even report the Women's Super League matches half the time!"

Hannah motioned for her to sit down, then turned to Kriss. "Send Gemma our love and tell her to come back when she's ready."

Kriss nodded. "Thanks. I'm sure she'll appreciate it." He gave me a quick smile before he and Hannah headed towards the door. Amy hurried after them. I wanted to do the same but I didn't feel I had the right. Gemma isn't coming back, I kept saying to myself over and over. Gemma, my strike partner, my team-mate, my hero, was not coming back. And it was all my fault.

2

Parrs v. Misslecott Goldstars
(Nettie Honeyball Cup quarter final)

That Saturday morning, everything seemed the same but felt wrong. My kit looked just the same when I put it on, but it felt wrong. My mum wished me luck and that felt wrong. At the ground everyone greeted me in the same way and that felt wrong. I'd expected someone to have a go at me for what had happened with Gemma but no one did. In fact, no one mentioned Gemma at all, not even Amy. It was as if everyone had made a conscious decision not to. I found it all a bit strange and it was a relief when it was time for kick-off.

☆ ☆ ☆

Misslecott Goldstars were not the strongest
opposition in the world. Even without our star
player we had the most possession and dominated
play. Nika, playing centre-mid, selflessly provided
me with plenty of goal-scoring opportunities, but
could I score? Even at close range? Could I, heck!
It was as if my feet had been fixed to the grass with
tent pegs.

My marker couldn't believe her luck. She nipped
the ball away every time without the slightest
resistance from me. True, she didn't know what
to do with the ball once she had it but that was
beside the point. As the minutes ticked by, I became
more and more rooted to the spot. Things went
from feeling wrong to feeling freaky. When Hannah
swapped me over I couldn't wait to get off the pitch.
"Please score and put me out of my misery," I told
JJ as she took my place.

"Will do," she replied.

Sure enough, two minutes later, she put us

one–nil up. "I'm glad someone knows what they're doing," I said to Tabinda.

I hoped my half-time snack of an apple and half a bar of fruit-and-nut might sort me out, but when Hannah put me on again midway through the second half I was even more feeble than in the first. I don't think I would have scored if the Goldstars had all gone for a tea-break and sent the goalie to the shops for the biscuits.

Luckily, Nika was way more alert and scored twice from JJ's corners and the match ended three–nil to us.

We were through to the semifinals of the Nettie Honeyball Cup.

When I got home, instead of writing the score next to the fixture like I usually did, I folded the paper over so I couldn't see the Misslecott listing at all, even though we'd won. I didn't want any reminders of that one. Then I checked on the website and saw we'd be playing the Tembridge Vixens in the semifinal, so I pencilled that in the space designated "Cup weekend". It meant that at least the list hadn't shrunk, even if my skills had.

CUDDLETHORPE TIGERS (AWAY)

GROVE BELLES (AWAY)

SOUTHFIELDS ATHLETIC (HOME)

CUP WEEKEND – NETTIE HONEYBALL CUP SEMIFINAL GROUP "A":

~~TEAMS TBC~~ TEMBRIDGE VIXENS V. PARRS

LUTTON ASH ANGELS (HOME)

3

On Monday, I bumped into Megan as I was wheeling the Year Six music trolley back to its cupboard in the hall. She was already in there, returning her Year Five's. "Good result on Saturday, eh?" she said.

"Well, apart from me playing like a plank."

She shrugged. "Yeah, you had a 'mare but you're bound to be a bit rubbish without Gemma at first. You'll be cushty next week."

I gawped at her.

"What?"

"You mentioned Gemma."

"So?"

"You didn't on Saturday, not once."

"No point, was there? She wasn't playing. A captain has to focus on the team she's got on the day."

"I guess."

"I'm treating it like she's got an injury. You know, missing a couple of matches with a hamstring problem. Maybe you should look at it like that, too? It might help."

I shrugged. I didn't think it would, somehow.

Megan picked up a drumstick and beat out a quick rhythm on a nearby steel pan. "Cheer up, Akky. It wasn't your fault. Any one of us could have recognized him and taken that photo."

"I know but…"

"What happened happened. She'll be back, don't you worry."

"Will she?"

"For sure. Football's in her blood. We've just got to give her time, like her dad said. Besides, something big's going to happen to us this season, with or without Hursty, I just know it is."

"You think so?"

"I know so!" She beamed.

As it turned out, Megan was right, something

big did happen, at training the next evening. Unfortunately, I don't think it was quite what she had in mind.

I had arrived early. "You all right there, Evo?" Hannah greeted me as soon as she saw me. "Katie and I are just going to have a quick meeting. We'll be in the storeroom if anybody needs us."

"Roger that, coach," I replied.

A minute later Holly, Nika and the twins arrived, followed by Mr Cutts the caretaker. "Who's in charge round here?" he asked. "Someone's car alarm's going off and it's sending the missus nuts."

I padded across to the storeroom to fetch Hannah and Katie. The door was ajar and I was about to knock when something about the way Hannah and Katie were talking held me back. "You have to tell them," Katie was saying in an anxious tone.

"I can't!" Hannah replied. "You do it."

"It's better coming from you."

"Maybe we should leave it?"

"Han, we said we'd do it this week, so let's do it. They'll be fine. Winning on Saturday will have given them a boost."

"You're right," Hannah whispered. "I'm dreading how they'll react, though."

I frowned. React to what?

The door flew open before I had a chance to look innocent. "Eve!" Hannah said, her cheeks turning pink.

"Um ... a car alarm is sending Mrs Cutts nuts."

"Mrs Cutts went nuts years ago." Katie chuckled. "I'll go and sort it."

Hannah put her arm around my shoulder. "Come on, then, Akky. Let's get cracking."

Well, of course I couldn't have cracked an egg after that. I was too distracted, wondering what they were dreading so much.

We had our drills as usual but when it was time to play our match at the end, Hannah clapped her hands and called for our attention. "Right, girls, warm down, then I need you all over to the benches, please."

"Warm down? Aren't we having a match?" Lucy asked.

"Not tonight. I need to talk to you all about something instead," Hannah said.

The whole of my spine tingled. Here it comes, I thought.

Hannah definitely had something important to say. I could tell from the way she was sitting, her arms clasped round her knees, thumb-tips tapping against each other. I sat up straight, alert and curious. "Could those of you who are going to secondary in September raise your hands?" she asked. Holly, Amy, Lucy, Nika and little old me shoved our hands in the air. There would have been another hand but … you know. "Yep. That's half the team ineligible for the Under 11s league next season. The first thing we should talk about is that."

"We need new players," Tabinda said.

"We could ask around," Megan suggested.

"That's how we got the team together in the first place. Just by asking…"

Lucy raised her hand again. "Couldn't we all just become an Under 12s team? I don't want to leave the Parrs."

I stared at Lucy in admiration. That's what you call a genius idea. No wonder she was always top of the class.

"Well, it's a possibility, I suppose," Hannah replied. She paused and glanced across at Katie. "Thing is, whatever happens, Katie and I can't coach you."

It took a second for eleven brains to ask the same question: did she just say what I thought she said? Then, when the brains all said, "Yes, she did," there was uproar.

"We're really sorry," Hannah continued hastily. "We've loved every second with you all but we can't take you any further…"

"Why not?" several people asked at once.

Megan, sitting opposite me, looked as if she'd

been kicked by a kangaroo. Hannah addressed her when she replied, "Because I'm going to teacher training college in September and Katie's backpacking across Australia. Neither of us is going to be here."

"We wanted to tell you now," Katie continued, "so it didn't come as a shock at the end of the season and to give you a chance to decide what you wanted to do next."

Jenny-Jane decided what she wanted to do next. "I might have known you'd bail out on us!" she yelled, walking backwards in fury towards the exit. "I might have known! How come all the best people leave and the ones you can't stand never do? Eh? How come?"

I glanced across at Amy. Exactly, I thought.

4

Parrs v. Cuddlethorpe Tigers (away)

As you can imagine, the atmosphere before kick-off at the next match was so subdued you'd have thought we'd all been tranquilized. Jenny-Jane was the worst, choosing to stand apart from everyone and scowl for Britain.

As for the match itself, it makes me cringe to think about it. We were so bad! Bad at the back, bad in midfield and bad up front. Bad, bad, bad. Hannah and Katie kept looking at each other in despair, knowing their news had hit us hard. Even easy-going team-mates like Nika were affected. "What are you doing?" she snapped when I ended up alongside her for the umpteenth time, leaving the left wing empty.

I looked around, confused. Gemma would have instinctively switched sides, but Nika and I didn't have the same connection. "Um…"

"Go back to your own bit!"

But two minutes later I was treading on her boots again. "Eve! Go away, will you!" she hissed.

Hannah tried to make a joke of it at half-time. We were a mere *four*–nil down then. She put her hand against her forehead and squinted into the distance. "Hello? Has anyone seen our striker?" she asked.

I resented being singled out. OK, I'd been rubbish but no more rubbish than anyone else. Without thinking, I put my hand against my forehead and went, "Yes … she's over there waiting for a decent cross into the box!"

I didn't mean it and I wouldn't have said it if I'd known Nika was right behind me. She just carried on towards the pile of coats and bags but she must have heard.

"That's not like you, Eve," Katie said.

Tell me about it.

In the second half they subbed me for Amy.

"What?" Amy said. "Me? You're putting me on?" She had to be the only player I knew who didn't like coming off the bench.

"Her? You might as well put a lump of lard up front," Jenny-Jane spat.

"Her" gave JJ a "haughty princess" special. "Don't you dare compare me to lard! If I am anything from the world of fats and spreads I am Olivio, thank you very much," Amy declared and swept on to the pitch. Despite myself I grinned. That was a quality comeback.

There was no quality comeback from the Parrs, though, and we let in another three goals. Megan threw her gloves to the ground in disgust and stormed off at the end of the match, not talking to any of us.

When I got home I couldn't bear to write that score on the fixture list either so I did what I did last time and folded the sheet over. The trouble was there was no extra match to add this time. The list was shrinking. And not in a good way.

GROVE BELLES (AWAY)

SOUTHFIELDS ATHLETIC (HOME)

CUP WEEKEND – NETTIE MONEYBALL CUP SEMIFINAL GROUP "A":

~~TEAMS TBC~~ TEMBRIDGE VIXENS V. PARRS

LUTTON ASH ANGELS (HOME)

5

On Monday, I bumped into Megan in the music cupboard again. This time we were both as glum as each other. "All right?" she asked despondently, wheeling her trolley into the corner next to mine.

"Yeah. You?"

"S'pose."

We both sighed at the same time and turned to leave, only to find the door blocked by Mr Glasshouse, our head teacher. "Ah! Excellent. I couldn't have hoped for two more reliable assistants." And he began reading from a list in his booming voice. "I need maracas, castanets and xylophones for Noisy Worship. Any idea where they are, girls?"

I wafted a hand towards the plastic tubs by

the wall. "Over there, sir. Do you want me to pass them across?"

"Thank you," he began, then stopped. "What's the matter? You both look like you've lost a pound and found a penny, as my granny used to say."

Megan and I exchanged glances and shrugged.

"Let me guess. The beautiful game was not beautiful over the weekend?"

I handed him the box of castanets. "Got it in one."

"Heavy loss?"

"Seven–nil," Megan grunted.

"Everyone loses now and again, Megan. Look upon it as a learning experience."

"Whatever." It was plain she was in no mood for teacher-talk.

"It's not just that we lost, Mr Glasshouse; it's why we lost," I told him and explained about Gemma and Hannah and Katie (although I left out the bit about why Gemma had dropped out of the team. I just said she was our best player).

He was a bit more understanding then but not

much. "Hmm. That is bad luck but it's par for the course these days. Players leave. Coaches leave. All you can do is pick yourself up and get on with it."

"But when players leave they're usually replaced by other players. Same with coaches. We've got nobody!" Megan complained. "Not that anybody could replace Hannah," she added. To my astonishment her bottom lip began to tremble.

Mr Glasshouse pretended to drop the box of castanets in shock. "What's this? Megan Fawcett upset because of a couple of minor mishaps? Where's the girl who challenged me to put her in the school team because she wanted to be keeper for England? Where's the girl who set up her own team? Where's my feisty Fawcett?" Megan's cheeks turned the colour of her hair as Mr Glasshouse continued. "You're the captain. You should be rallying the troops, not crumbling under a bit of pressure. Am I right or am I right?" He strode off, forgetting his maracas but calling out over his shoulder, "IT Suite's free at break."

We both watched him stride across the hall, then Megan turned to me, her eyes glinting. "You heard the man. IT Suite at break! Team meeting. Tell Nika and Lucy."

"Roger that, captain," I said, saluting her.

Given that she'd had hardly any time to prepare, Megan did a brilliant job of rallying. When I arrived in the IT Suite with Nika and Lucy half an hour later she was already pacing up and down the small space between the computer consoles like an army general. She immediately apologized for her behaviour on Saturday. "I was out of order storming off like that. I let you down and I let myself down."

"We were all as bad," Petra reasoned.

Megan nodded. "I know. That's what I want to talk about." She glanced across at me. "Losing players and coaches is par for the course. We just have to get on with it. Gemma might come back, but if she doesn't we've got Nika, JJ and Tabinda in midfield, who are as skilled as anyone in the league. As for Hannah and Katie..." She paused as her voice broke. "At least we've got them until the end of the season. Throwing the towel in now is no way to thank them for all they've done for us."

"Done for us? Like dumping us, you mean?" JJ grunted.

Megan stopped dead. "Don't even go there, Bayliss. They've done more for you than anybody, so I'd zip it if I were you."

JJ looked so startled at being told off by someone who, let's face it, is usually soft with her, that she didn't utter another word. Megan took up her pacing again. "I know we've lost a bit of spark lately but we can still go out on a high, can't we? I don't mean winning the league or the cup – I'm not bothered about stuff like that any more – I just want us to be united for our last few matches…"

"Especially when one of the last few matches is against Grove Belles," I said, remembering my list. In case you don't know, the Belles are our nemesis team. We've only beaten them once and that was at the beginning of the season when they were adjusting to the loss of their experienced players such as Bend it like Becky. A lump came to my throat. That would be the Parrs next season. Adjusting without me.

"Not the Ding Dong Belles!" Dylan called out. "When? When?"

"This Saturday," Megan replied. "No way are we going to let them walk all over us. We've got to play well against them. For Hannah and Katie."

"For Hannah and Katie!" Dylan and Daisy repeated and began racing around the room until Mr Glasshouse turfed us out for making too much noise. Cheek!

6

Megan's fighting talk cheered me up so much I arrived at after-school club singing my favourite jingle from a Dr Pepper advert. I sang it all the way through setting up the baking table for Mrs Rose and I was still singing it twenty minutes later when Amy arrived.

"Someone's happy," she said as she passed by on her way to the book corner.

"Someone is!" I beamed, forgetting we weren't speaking.

She must have forgotten, too, because she hesitated, then pulled out a chair and sat next to me. "So what's with the singing?"

"I'm feeling inspired," I told her and filled her in about the meeting.

Her face dropped. "Great. The Mowborough Massive strikes again."

"What do you mean?"

"I don't suppose you lot think that I might like to be involved in your little team-talk meetings?"

I scowled. "How can you? You go to a different school."

"So what? That's not my fault, is it?" she said with an annoyed flick of her hair. "It's not just me. Holly feels the same. You lot are always so cliquey."

"No we aren't! We don't normally hang out together at school at all. I don't even talk to Lucy and Nika that much and we're in the same class. But this is different, isn't it? We're in an emergency situation."

Her tone softened then. She hitched closer. "You mean with Gemma?"

"More Hannah and Katie," I admitted.

"Oh. Of course." For such a short sentence she managed to put an awful lot of sarcasm into it.

"What's that supposed to mean?" I asked,

growing annoyed. "I miss Gemma as much as you do, you know. More, probably."

"More? How'd you work that one out? She's my best friend, not yours."

"Not on the pitch, she isn't," I mumbled.

"Really? You've got a funny way of showing it." With that, Amy took herself off to the book corner and ignored me, not just for the rest of the afternoon but for the rest of the week.

So much for Megan's dream of a united team.

7

Parrs v. Grove Belles (away)

On Saturday morning, I dressed quickly and trundled down the stairs, still yawning.

Ashtonby is miles away, so it's an early start.

Mum, as usual, was already up and asked what I wanted for breakfast. "Cereal's fine," I muttered, not feeling particularly hungry. Mum frowned. She likes breakfasts to be of the cooked variety.

"Eve?"

"Mum?"

"You've got a face as long as a ski slope. I hope you aren't still fretting over this thing with Gemma? Because what happened wasn't your fault. You do know that, don't you?"

Try telling Amy Minter that, I thought.

"It isn't," Mum repeated. "Now, porridge or beans on toast?"

I sighed and opted for beans on toast, and after that it was rush, rush, rush while Mum tried to finish a thousand jobs before setting off. By the time we arrived at Ashtonby we had only minutes to spare. "I'm sorry I can't stay to watch," Mum apologized. "Asda calls."

"No worries." The way I was playing, the fewer witnesses the better.

She gave me a massive hug and wished me luck.

"I'll need it," I told her and hurried across the grass to join my team-mates.

Because I was late, Hannah had left me out of the starting line-up and I found myself stranded on the touchline with Petra and Amy. I didn't mind Petra, but I hadn't spoken to Amy since our exchange at after-school club, and judging by the determined way she was staring ahead that wasn't about to change any time soon.

Petra squeezed my arm tight. "We'd better do well," she agonized. "Megan is going to be unbearable if we don't."

"I know. She'll probably haul us in for another meeting," I joked.

"And you can't have too many of those, can you?" Amy muttered.

"We're off! We're off!" Petra squealed before I could tell Amy to get lost.

With that I focused on the pitch.

We started brightly enough. "Well in!" Katie kept shouting as we fought for every ball. The Belles kept pressing, but Holly and Lucy were defending well and Megan had that defiant look on her face that said "Score if you dare."

"We are stormin 'em!" Petra grabbed Amy's arm.

"Hello? Trying to text," Amy told her.

Petra rolled her eyes at me but I just shrugged. What Amy did was none of my business.

Although there was no doubt we were playing a hundred per cent better than last week, we kept losing the ball in midfield. Nika, Tabinda and JJ were trying hard but they didn't have Gemma's ability to prise open the defence. Still, the half ended nil–nil, which was impressive, considering. Hannah was delighted. "Awesome! Awesome!" she kept repeating. I smiled. Hannah would think we were awesome if we lost 20–0. That's why we all loved her.

I was selected for the start of the second half. "Eve on for JJ," Hannah ordered. "Amy on for Tabs, Petra for Holly."

Perhaps the Belles had been given a blasting by their coach at half-time, or maybe they knew Hannah's everyone-gets-a-go policy, too. Either way, they came out roaring and scored within two minutes because their striker was able to swerve round Petra more easily than Holly and so slot the ball beyond Megan's reach. "Head up, Meggo! Push on, Parrs, push on," Katie urged as we walked back to the centre spot.

☆ ☆ ☆

We pushed on. I fell back into midfield to support them but I wasn't much use. The tent pegs for feet had returned. When a great goal kick from Megan landed near me I couldn't budge. "That's yours, Eve!" Katie shouted. Luckily, Nika decided it was hers, got to it before their defender did and worked it all the way to the edge of the box before their number two, a lanky girl with fair hair and a bright red fringe, tackled her and booted the ball out for a corner.

We'd practised corners a lot lately, and I took my place at the near post. I was tall and knew my height would block the goalie's vision. I watched, heart thumping, as Nika raised her left hand. That meant she was going to cross it towards me. As the ball headed in my direction, I prepared to jump, ignoring all the jostling I could feel going on behind me. I was focused on the ball, thinking this was it, my chance to make up for the last couple of games, but before I could do anything the whistle blew. I looked behind me. Amy was writhing on the ground, her eyes squeezed shut in pain. At first I thought she might be acting – I wouldn't put it past her – but Hannah's concern was real enough as she helped Amy hobble off.

"It was her!" Jenny-Jane called out, pointing to one of the defenders. "She gave her a dead leg, didn't she."

"I never!" the defender retorted.

"You take it, Eve," Katie ordered.

For a moment I didn't realize what she meant until I saw the referee nodding at me and pointing to the spot. Penalty.

I took a steadying breath, stepped back two, three, four paces, then I did something stupid. I looked around for Gemma to give me a bit of moral support, but of course she wasn't there. I knew then I'd miss – and I did. You should have seen that ball blaze over the crossbar. Terrific.

After that I went from sluggish to slug. I barely moved. From the corner of my eye, I saw Katie signalling to Hannah. Seconds later Dylan was put on in my place. How bad is that? Being subbed for one of the Psycho twins?

"Are you OK?" Hannah asked as I trudged off the field.

I slapped on my happy face. "Course I am! The Belles paid me twenty quid to miss that penalty. Think how much chocolate I can get with that!"

"You daft bat!" Hannah said, shaking her head. "Go and sit with Amy for a minute."

I glanced over Hannah's shoulder to where Amy was sitting on an orange plastic chair; her leg propped up on a bag of balls. "Do I have to?"

"Course you have to. It's what team-mates do."

This should be interesting, I thought as I headed towards her.

8

I began with a curt, "Yo."

Amy replied with a curt, "Hey", but immediately followed it with, "Check this out." Then she pulled a bag of ice from her thigh and showed me a large red mark.

"Nasty."

"I love it! I've never had a sports injury before. I can't wait to tell Gemma."

I gazed across at the game. "I wish she was here now. She always loved playing the Belles."

"Did she?"

"Well, dur!"

Amy shrugged. "You know me. I totally zoned out when the pair of you talked football."

"Yeah. You're not exactly what you'd call a

sports enthusiast, are you? I'm surprised you still turn up."

"What with me being so useless."

I felt my cheeks singe. It sounded bad when she put it like that. "Kind of."

She shrugged. "I have to turn up. I'm the link between Gemma and the Parrs, aren't I? Lose that and we lose her."

"That's a bit big-headed, isn't it?"

Amy threw down the ice pack in exasperation and glared at me. "You just don't get it, do you? If I don't get her to play again she's letting the fear win, and if the fear wins she's never going to get over being kidnapped, is she? Don't you ever read the problem pages?"

I felt as if Amy had thrown the ice pack at me instead of the ground. Of course. How had I missed that? I nodded, to show I understood.

"Finally!" Amy reached out her hand. I pulled her up and we began to walk towards the touchline, her arm slotted through mine for support.

"But how can we get her to play if she won't come to matches or anything?"I asked.

"That's the problem. I don't know. I was hoping you might help me come up with something, seeing as you're the one who's got that dream-team thing going with her."

"Had."

She sighed. "Had, but could have again if we work together. Look, how about we meet at after-school club on Monday? To talk about it?"

"Sure. I'd like that."

"Me, too."

A look of understanding passed between us, then Amy unhooked herself and limped towards our pile of coats and bags. I joined Tabinda on the touchline just as the final whistle blew. That was it. We'd lost one–nil to Grove Belles thanks to my missed penalty.

At home I folded another match out of sight and sighed. As you can see, the list was disappearing faster than a puddle in a desert.

Southfields Athletic (home)

Cup weekend – Nettie Honeyball Cup semifinal group "A":

~~Teams TBC~~ Tembridge Vixens v. Parrs

Lutton Ash Angels (home)

9

I spent all Saturday evening and the whole of Sunday trying to figure out how to persuade Gemma to return, but everything I came up with – like phoning or writing – had already drawn a blank. Still, the last thing I wanted was to turn up at after-school club empty-handed. I wanted to prove to Amy that I could bring something to the table, even if it was only a few sandwiches. But by Monday I was still waiting for inspiration, so I did what any Parr would do and called for back-up.

For once that Monday morning it was me, not Megan, who arranged a meeting with the Mowborough Massive. "Will this take long?" Petra wanted to know as we gathered in the IT Suite again. "Only I've got drama club in ten minutes."

Eight heads swivelled in my direction. I was nervous, so I started off with a long-winded introduction. "Ladies and gentlemen, boys and girls, socceroos, dudes and dudesses…" I caught Megan's eye. *Be serious,* her expression read. I stopped and cleared my throat. "OK. You all know I've been mega diabolical recently. Missing penalties and little things like that."

"Yes," everyone chorused.

"Well, apart from penalties, the thing I'm missing most is Gemma. I really want her to come back. Plus, she needs to come back. For her own sake."

Amy's reasoning didn't seem to have the same impact on the rest of the team as it had had on me. In fact, I was surprised to see a few shrugs. "No one forced her to leave the team," Megan pointed out.

"I know, but she's confused. She needs our help."

"We tried to help. We sent her letters and cards with loads of hearts and kisses, but she didn't reply," Daisy said.

"Yes but…"

"And we've all got problems, haven't we?" JJ interrupted. "It doesn't stop us coming to football."

"But Gemma's problems are *because* of football!' I said, growing exasperated.

There was a frosty silence. This meeting was not playing out at all like it had in my head. Everyone was meant to come up with loads of ideas for me to take to Amy, not argue with me.

Lucy tried to soothe things over. "Look, Eve. We all want Gemma back as much as you do, but we've been told to back off by her dad and Hannah, so that's what we're doing."

"But Amy says—" I began but Petra stood up to leave before I could finish and soon everyone was shuffling and gathering bags.

"One thing before you all go..." Megan said, reclaiming the floor. I sagged with relief, assuming she was going to come out with one of her stirring we're-all-in-this-together speeches but no. "We need to start thinking about a leaving present for Hannah and Katie," she said instead and was immediately greeted with way more positive reactions than I'd got.

Megan smiled. "Cool. Any volunteers to collect money and stuff?"

"Why don't you ask Amy or Holly to do it?" I suggested, remembering what Amy had said about us being cliquey but not thinking for one minute Megan would agree.

To my surprise, she nodded. "Minty. I'll leave it to you to tell them, then, yeah?"

"No problem," I mumbled.

So that's how the meeting ended, with me feeling deflated and with the added bonus that I'd landed Amy and Holly a job they probably didn't want. Another Akboh mess-up.

10

"Um … how's your leg?" I asked the moment Amy stepped through the door at after-school club.

"Better," she replied. She hung up her blazer in the cloakroom then raised her eyebrows. "What?"

"What do you mean 'what?'"

"You're hovering. You never hover."

"I have a confession to make," I told her. "Actually, two confessions."

"Don't tell me. You've eaten a deep-fried Mars bar and thrown up in the book corner?"

"Worse…"

"You've thrown up on Mrs Rose?"

I frowned. "Will you leave it out with the throwing-up stuff?"

She grinned and headed into the main room,

signed in, turfed two kids out of the book corner and then looked at me. "Well?"

I took a deep breath and described what a downer the meeting had been. "I got nowhere," I admitted miserably.

"Of course you didn't. They're putting the needs of the team before the needs of the individual."

"Are they?"

"It's a classic dilemma in competitive situations."

"Is it?"

"Of course it is. You only have to watch one episode of *Junior Apprentice* to know that. And the second confession?"

I was so bamboozled by the "needs of the team" gubbins that she had to repeat the question.

"Right! The second confession," I said. This time I spoke so fast I sounded like I'd been inhaling helium gas all day, then squeezed my eyes shut.

I expected at least a heavy sigh or a "Well, that's just typical" but when I opened one eye, Amy had this humungous grin on her face. "That's brilliant!"

"Is it?"

"Gemma adores Hannah and Katie. I know she'd want to join in with this."

"You think?"

Amy nodded, her face filled with the same light that I've seen in the eyes of old ladies at church when the spirit moves them. "Definitely. This is the subtle thing we needed. Go, Eve! All we need to do now is plan the meetings. We should have them here, on neutral territory."

"Are you sure she'll come? With me being here?"

"Eve, how many more times? This isn't about you! Gemma only stopped coming to after-school club because she needed some space to get her head together. That meant cutting out all the things she didn't have to do so she could concentrate on the bits she did have to do, like go to school."

That made sense. Although I hated to admit it, Amy really did know Gemma better than me. "Wow, Amy. Are you going to be a psychologist when you grow up?" I asked her.

"No. I'm going to be a businesswoman like my mum and Karren Brady. Now, about the meetings. I'll invite Holly too. It will look less suspicious."

"Good call."

"And don't mess up by talking football."

"I won't," I promised.

"Let's start on the gift ideas now," she said, plunging into her retro leather satchel and pulling out a notebook. She began to jot things down in neat columns, looking up only occasionally to frown, cross something out and then add something else. I just sat there, staring in admiration, realizing I was watching a maestro at work.

11

I was sure Amy wouldn't be able to persuade Gemma to come to after-school club but what did I know? On Tuesday Amy declared she'd done the selling job of her life, and on Wednesday, miracle of miracles, Gemma arrived. She seemed nervous, but then I wasn't doing an impression of a cool cucumber myself. First she glanced around, like a holidaymaker returning home to check everything was where she'd left it, and then she looked at me.

We stared at each other for about ten seconds before doing that thing of talking at the same time, which sounded funny and broke the ice. It helped having Holly there, too, especially as she was an after-school club newbie. The three of us focused on making her feel welcome. The even number balanced us out, too, and even if it hadn't, Amy wasn't going to give us time to dwell on anything. "Here you go," she said, producing a badge for each of us.

We squinted at each other's labels. Holly was Graphics, Gemma was Researcher, Amy was Chief Buyer and I was Liaison Officer. "Liaison Officer? What's that?" I asked.

The Chief Buyer guffawed. "Hello! You liaise! You are the link between the committee and the others. You collect the money, update them with decisions and stuff like that."

"I'm not allowed money in school."

"No worries. You hand it over to Tracie and she keeps it until we need it."

"She's already offered," Holly confirmed.

"Neat," I said, grinning at Holly. Tracie, Holly's stepmum, is our lunchtime supervisor. How handy is that?

Amy continued. "Right. I've spoken to Megan. She reckons the handover of the gifts should be at the presentation evening in May, so that only gives us six weeks. It's going to be a push but we'll cope." She began dishing out lists and printouts and magazines and gel pens.

"Um ... before we start, can you show me where the loos are?" Holly asked.

"Follow me," Amy said.

While we waited for them to return I found myself so overwhelmed that Gemma was actually sitting opposite me that I couldn't think of a thing to say. Actually, that's a fib. I could think of plenty I wanted to say, like how dreadful I felt about the whole photo episode and how shocked I was when I heard about the kidnapping and how rubbish I'd been playing without her, but I didn't dare say any of it. I knew I'd scare her right off and then we'd be back to square one. Or minus square one because Amy would have killed me. "Nice to have you back," I managed instead.

Her cheeks flushed. "Nice to be back," she replied.

12

Parrs v. Southfields Athletic (home)

What a difference a few days makes!

I bounded out of bed that Saturday morning and almost snapped the pulley right off when I opened my bedroom blinds. "Good morning, wonderful world!" I called out, then galloped downstairs.

"What's with you, Hyper Girl?" Claude asked when I entered the kitchen letting rip with a few funky dance moves. "You been on the Nutella?"

"She can't have. I polished it off last night," Samuel informed us.

"Excuse me, brothers, but not all my happiness is chocolate related."

"Since when?" Claude asked as I reached for the

Coco Pops (Mum was out – it was safe to do so).

"FYI, I'm happy because I'm friends with Gemma again."

"Cool."

"Is she back in the team, then?" Samuel asked.

"Not yet, but me and Amy are working on it."

Claude stood up and began to clear his breakfast things from the table. "Hope so. I felt bad over what happened with Marlon. She's quality. It would be criminal for her not to play any more."

I nodded. There was no arguing with that.

"How's it going with Hursty?" Megan asked the second I arrived at the ground.

"Splendid," I replied. As Liaison Officer, I'd been keeping everyone informed about our progress and Megan was naturally taking a keen interest.

"Any chance she'll be back for the semifinal against the Vixens?"

"Well…" I began, but Amy arrived out of nowhere and grabbed me.

"With regret we are unable to give a precise date at this moment in time," she told Megan before whisking me away.

"What did you do that for?"

"Because I know you. You'll say something silly like 'For sure she's coming back' when she's nowhere near ready yet."

"Sorry," I apologized because she was right, I would have. But my insides were fizzing. Gemma would come back soon. She would. She had to.

Meanwhile I was feeling much more confident about my football. Just seeing my old partner again had geed me up so much. "Put me on first, please. Pretty please," I begged Hannah (and I mean begged – I was down on one knee).

"Get up, you daft doughnut." She laughed but she did put me on first. Result!

As I waited for kick-off I could feel the adrenalin pump through me. This was it, I thought, taking in huge gulps of air, This was what it was all about. I looked up at the sky. Wish me luck, Dad.

Then the whistle blew and it was game on. Poor Southfields. They had always been the whipping boys (or girls) of the league and today was no different. The score at half-time was nine–one to us. I'd like to report I scored a few of those nine but I didn't. Still, at least I'd vanquished the tent pegs and was running with the ball way better.

Close to the end of the first half I almost pulled off a great one–two with Nika, but my shot glanced off the post. Our supporters "ooh"ed at that one. When I saw Hannah clapping my effort I put my hand to my forehead and said, "Has anyone seen our striker?" to save her doing it.

Hannah just laughed and told me, "You're getting there."

Before the start of the second half she called us all together. "If we win I don't want any silly celebrations at the end. Southfields get thumped every week. Think about how they feel," she whispered.

We did win – 14–2 – but we remembered what Hannah had said. We just stood still and waited as their captain called for three cheers for us. It came out as a half-hearted, defeated mumble. But when it was our turn, not only did we give them three rousing cheers, we clapped them off the pitch.

"What you doing this for?" a girl called Crystal asked me. "Are you being sarcastic?"

"No," I told her. "We're doing it because you deserve it for never giving up."

She shrugged. "What a bunch of weirdos."

Charming. There's no pleasing some people!

When I filled in the Southfields score that night, my joy at the win evaporated. Look at the fixture list, dude! You have to squint to even see it!

SOUTHFIELDS ATHLETIC (HOME)   14–2

CUP WEEKEND – NETTIE MONEYBALL CUP SEMIFINAL GROUP "A":

~~TEAMS TBC~~ TEMBRIDGE VIXENS v. PARRS

LUTTON ASH ANGELS (HOME)

Two tiny matches left. TWO. Time was running out. For all of us.

13

Luck was on our side in one way. Because of the bad winter, a lot of teams were behind with their league fixtures. The Tembridge Vixens had been particularly badly affected and had asked for the date of the semifinal to be put back twice while they worked through their outstanding games. The extra time gave us more free Saturdays than we'd expected. It was what to do with one of the free Saturdays that led to an unexpected development at after-school club. "Isn't it great we've got another Saturday free? I'm hitting the shops. What are you guys doing?" Amy asked.

Gemma, who had a bit of a cold, blew her nose. "If I'm feeling OK I'm going with my dad to Cannock Chase."

Holly grinned. "I'm going to watch City with my dad. They're away to Leeds."

I didn't reply. Usually I'm fine when people talk about what they're doing with their dads but every now and then I get a stab of jealousy that jabs me right in the gut. I felt the stab then. I would have given anything to spend a day with my dad in real life instead of at a graveside.

I pretended I was concentrating on my project. After a few seconds the spasm faded and I looked up, only to find everyone staring at me, waiting for an answer. "Um ... the usual," I mumbled. "Chores and things."

Amy smiled. "Cool. OK, I want to check out my budget spreadsheets on the computer. Holly, coming?"

After they'd gone Gemma put her hand on my arm. "Are you OK?" she asked quietly.

"Me? Sure. Why shouldn't I be?"

"You looked a bit sad. Was it because we were talking about our dads?"

My stomach knotted. "Nah. Too much cornflake tart at lunchtime. That fourth portion was just one slab too far."

"You're fibbing, I can tell."

"Can you?"

"Uh-huh. I recognize that look. I remember it from when we were making cards for Father's Day and you said to Mrs Rose, 'Yo, dude, what's the girl with the dead dad meant to do?' You had that same look on your face just now you had then. Like it hurt but you were trying not to show it."

Our eyes locked. "OK," I said. "I admit it hurts sometimes."

"Do you remember your dad much?"

"I was nearly six. Course I do."

"It must have been awful when he died."

"No. It was great."

"I'm sorry," she apologized, thinking I was being sarcastic.

"I mean it," I reassured her. "He was so poorly it was a mercy."

Gemma seemed uncomfortable when I said that. I get that a lot. People who start to ask questions about dead people don't really like it when you answer too truthfully. "And I knew he was in heaven, so that helped," I continued anyway. "It's the best place to be, isn't it? Hanging out with Jesus and Bob Marley. It doesn't get any better than that."

"If you believe in that kind of thing…"

"I totally do. I would never have managed going to school the day after he died otherwise."

Gemma gasped. "You went to school the next day? That's so brave."

"I was just carrying on as normal. Claude and Samuel did the same. Besides, we'd promised Dad we'd get a good education. We weren't about to break our promise on day one."

"I couldn't have done that. No way."

"Course you could."

She lowered her eyes and shook her head. "I couldn't. I'm not like you. I'm not that tough."

"I'm not tough. I cried enough to fill ten buckets in class."

"Did everybody look?"

"No. They were busy crying too. I like to share!"

She smiled. "Typical Eve. Always the comedian."

I shrugged. "Why not? If I cried every time something got to me there'd be a world shortage of tissues."

"But what if … what if something's happened to someone who's not like that? Who can't joke about the bad things? What do they do?"

She dipped her head and began to draw a circle over and over again on her notepad. No need to ask what she was referring to.

I swallowed, knowing I had to tread carefully, which isn't easy with my big feet. "They have to find other ways of getting through it, I suppose."

"Such as?"

"Well, my mum keeps busy and…" I stopped. That was kind of all I'd got but Gemma was listening so intently you'd think I was Professor McGonagall or something. What else could I say? Unless I mentioned the Dr Pepper thing. "I have a thing I sometimes do," I said.

"What is it?"

I hesitated. "It's a bit lame."

"Go on."

"Well, do you remember that Dr Pepper advert that used to be on TV? The one that goes: 'What's the worst that could happen?'"

"I think so."

"I sing that when I get excited or nervous. I don't mean nervous about my dad so much but, you know, nervous about life things. Like going to the dentist or doing a maths test. I sing, 'What's the worst that could happen?' to myself, and that helps."

"I don't get it. How does that help?"

"Well, like if you take a test and you get two out of a hundred or something, what's the worst that could happen? You have to take the test again or you get told off by your teacher. But that's nothing, is it? Nobody locks you in a cell, right? Or makes you jump into a tank of piranhas."

"I suppose."

"And I know that no matter how embarrassing or scary or dreadful something seems it can't be anywhere near as bad as having someone you love die."

The pen in Gemma's hand stopped. "No. I guess not," she said, her voice little more than a whisper.

I waited a beat then added, "Though missing that penalty against Grove Belles came a close second."

Gemma lifted her head and gawped at me before bursting out laughing. "Eve! You're terrible."

"I know," I said. "But I'm terrible in a good way."

14

**Parrs v. Tembridge Vixens
(Nettie Honeyball Cup semifinal)**

**Things changed after the dead dad and
Dr Pepper conversation.** Gemma became way
more chatty and enthusiastic, not just about the
presentation evening but about everything. It was as
if she'd had her batteries changed and was radiating
energy again. Most of the time we talked about
school and homework and stuff like that, but then a
few days before the Vixens match Gemma asked us
if we'd been practising set pieces. I glanced across
at Amy and she raised her eyebrows to red alert.

"Yeah," Holly said. "Especially free kicks."

"You'll need to watch that ginger-haired striker.

She's fast," Gemma said.

"I know," Holly continued seamlessly. "Lucy's going to be marking her."

"Good. How's Megan? Is she getting all tense?" Gemma looked straight at me.

"Of course she is. Megan's Megan."

Gemma picked up a gel pen and smiled. "I love Megan. She's a proper captain. If I close my eyes I can hear her shouting."

"If you come to the match on Saturday you can hear her in real life."

Amy kicked me in the shin and I bit my lip, thinking I'd done my usual and gone too far. But Gemma just shrugged. "OK," she said.

"OK what?" I asked, just to double check.

"I'll come." She paused then added, "To watch. Nothing else."

And guess what? She did come, even though Amy kept telling me not to hold my breath because Gemma was famous for changing her mind at the last minute. She stood with her dad, her sister, Lizzie, and her dogs, Jake and Caspar, a little back from the rest of the spectators, trying to look inconspicuous. No chance. I'd warned everyone at school she might turn up and the second they saw her they galloped across the field to swamp her with hugs and high fives. Hannah had to call everyone back to warm up properly and give Gemma a chance to breathe.

"Well, it's a start, I suppose." Megan sighed as we walked back together towards the pile of coats and bags for our pre-match chat. "But I wish she'd brought her kit."

"Don't be like that," I told her. "Something good's going to happen today. I can feel it in my cornrows!" It was true, too. Just knowing Gemma was in the crowd had given me a buzz.

Megan tightened her bandana and turned to observe the Tembridge Vixens limbering up across the field. "I hope so. I don't think I can stand another depressing conversation with you and Mr Glasshouse in the music cupboard on Monday."

☆ ☆ ☆

As it happened, the next time we saw Mr Glasshouse it wasn't in the music cupboard but in assembly when he made all the Parrs stand up.

"And special mention must be made to Megan's girls' team, the Parrs, who are through to the Nettie Honeyball Cup Final. They beat the Tembridge Vixens in the semifinal on Saturday by … what was it, Megan?"

"Five–three," Megan announced proudly.

"And I believe someone scored a hat-trick?"

"Akky did, sir."

All eyes turned to me. "Well done, Eve," Mr Glasshouse said.

I grinned. "It would have been four but the wind was blowing in the wrong direction."

Everyone laughed, then Mr Glasshouse asked for a round of applause and wished us all good luck.

Lucy, standing next to me, leaned in and whispered, "We'll need it seeing as the final is against the Belles."

But I couldn't think that far ahead. I was too busy picturing not the first goal I'd headed in, or the second goal I'd slotted low in from a rebound, or even the third, which came thanks to a brilliant assist from Nika. Instead I pictured Gemma, who, as each goal had been scored, moved closer and closer to the touchline, clinging to a can of Dr Pepper and grinning from ear to ear.

And this is how the fixture list looked after I'd finished with it. Some people might think the lettering is a bit OTT, but I had to do *something* to pad the thing out.

SOUTHFIELDS ATHLETIC (HOME)   14—2

CUP WEEKEND — NETTIE HONEYBALL CUP SEMIFINAL GROUP "A":

~~TEAMS TBC~~ TEMBRIDGE VIXENS v. PARRS   5—3

LUTTON ASH ANGELS (HOME)

NETTIE HONEYBALL CUP FINAL:
GROVE BELLES v. PARRS

15

The next Tuesday at training felt strange.

It was our last official session before our last league match. I'd hoped Gemma would come along, but when I'd mentioned it at after-school club she'd shaken her head. "I can't, I'm ... er..."

"It's OK, you don't have to think up an excuse," I'd said as her cheeks flushed.

She'd looked at me gratefully. "I'll come and watch you play Lutton Ash, though. And I'll definitely be at the cup final. I wouldn't miss that for the world."

"I still wish she'd come to training," I told Amy as we sat on the benches later that evening. "Just so we could all be together."

"I know." Amy sighed. "But we did our best. And Gemma's mum told my mum she was amazed we'd managed to get her within a mile of the ground, never mind her staying the full length of the match last week. All in all, I think we've played a binder."

"A blinder."

"Whatever."

I guess she was right, but coming to training couldn't hurt, could it? I could have brought in a six pack of Dr Pepper! Still, like Amy said, we'd done our best.

Once we'd all arrived, Hannah began by discussing the Vixens game and telling us how proud she was of us. "So we're through to the final, eh? How awesome is that?"

We all cheered and the twins did their "We're on our way to Wembley, my knees have gone all tremble-y" dance.

Hannah moved on quickly before they got too giddy, saying she'd hand details of the final out later. "It's going to be held at Mowborough Park this year. There'll be other regional finals taking place at the same time, so it'll be quite a big event."

"You never know, we might even get into the *Mowborough Mercury*," Katie added.

Amy and I exchanged looks. Maybe it was just as well Gemma wouldn't be playing if the paper was going to be there.

"OK, let's crack on," Hannah said. "Who says we skip the drills and go straight for a match tonight? To celebrate getting to the final? With me and Katie joining in?"

"Yay!" everyone yelled.

"Thought you might like that! Warm up, then, girls..."

That turned into one of the best training sessions ever, with one side trying their best to score against Katie in goal and the other determined to win the ball off Hannah in midfield.

It was also one of the longest training sessions ever because nobody wanted to leave. All the parents ended up standing around at the back of the hall, fidgeting and checking their watches. "Giveus a break, you lot," Katie protested when we asked for yet another period of extra time. "Mr Cutts will have our guts for garters!"

"I'm beat," Hannah finally announced, pretending to collapse in a heap. "Take them away!" she begged our parents and then added, "But bring them back for the Lutton Ash match on Saturday!"

"Wear extra-strong shin pads," Megan warned. Lutton Ash Angels were a notoriously dirty team.

I sighed. Strange as it sounds I'd even miss playing them next year.

16

Parrs v. Lutton Ash Angels (home)

You'd think the last league match of the season would have had a bit of a party atmosphere but it was a real let-down. Lutton Ash only turned up with five players and we had to lend them Petra and Holly. It was against the rules, but if we hadn't we wouldn't have had a game at all. It finished 9–2 to us (I netted four, seeing as you asked). They got two goals but only because Megan let Petra, standing in as striker, score them.

"What's wrong with you lot? You've usually kicked us to pieces by now," I said to one of their defenders near the end.

She shrugged. "We're bottom of the league, aren't we? We've nothing to play for."

"You could at least try!" I said as the ball landed next to her and she just stood there. Even Gemma's dogs looked bored. I felt cheated, especially when they didn't even hang around for the three cheers at the end. I'd changed my mind. No way would I miss playing them next year!

"Give me Southfields any day," Megan mumbled as we headed for the changing rooms.

At home I stuck the final league table next to my list and wrote "Serves you right" next to Lutton Ash at the bottom.

I stared for ages at the single remaining fixture on my list: Nettie Honeyball Cup Final: Grove Belles v. Parrs. I was tempted to take the list down and draw around it and pimp it up a bit, but in the end I decided not to bother. No matter how large I made the font or how fancy I made the border, it wouldn't change the fact that this really was it. The final really would be my last match as a Parr.

Here's how the league table looked:

The Nettie Honeyball Women's Football League junior division

Team	P	W	D	L	Pts
Furnston Diamonds	18	11	4	3	37
Grove Belles	18	12	1	5	37
Tembridge Vixens	18	10	5	3	33
Parrs U11s	18	10	2	6	32
Greenbow United Girls	18	7	5	6	26
Misslecott Goldstars	18	6	5	7	23
Cuddlethorpe Tigers	18	6	2	10	20
Hixton Lees Juniors	18	5	4	9	19
Southfields Athletics	18	3	2	13	11
Lutton Ash Angels	18	2	1	15	7

17

It had been a while since I'd met Megan in the music cupboard. "Have you heard the good news?" she asked as we parked our trolleys.

"School news or Parrs news?"

"There is only one type of news, Eve. The rest is just stuff."

"Of course. What was I thinking? Parrs news, then."

"Tabinda can't play in the final. She has to go to a wedding in London. We'll manage, I suppose, but it's a pain. She's improved loads this year."

Then, on the Thursday before the match, there was more bad news. Daisy and Dylan had chicken pox. "Trust them to get something related to farm animals," Petra said.

Losing the twins wouldn't have mattered normally but losing the twins *and* Tabinda meant we were down to eight players. Megan passed a note across to our dinner table on Friday: NOBODY IS ALLOWED TO BE ILL OR GO TO WEDDINGS OR ANYTHING UNTIL SUNDAY AND THAT'S AN ORDER!

I kept the note and showed it to everyone at after-school club. Holly smiled. "My dad says Megan reminds him of Stuart Pearce."

"Why, does he have red curly hair and think he's it?" Amy asked.

"Not exactly," Holly replied. While she explained to Amy about the fiery ex-England player I watched Gemma read the note. "Scary, huh?" I said.

She scanned it quickly, then slid it back to me. "Well, remember what you told me. Ask yourself, 'What's the worst that can happen?'" she replied.

"What do you mean?"

"Even if you lose, nobody's going to lock you in a cell or chuck you into a tank full of piranhas."

Ouch. It looked like I'd done too good a job on her.

18

Parrs v. Grove Belles
The Nettie Honeyball Women's Football
League junior division Cup Final
Mowborough Park Ground
Kick-Off 2 p.m.

On Saturday, I sprang out of bed, strode across to the window, pulled up my blind and pulled it down again. It was so bright! Spring had finally sprung. I threw my kit on superfast and then threw it off again when I remembered the cup match wasn't until the afternoon. Doh! I had a whole morning to kill. I was so desperate to find something to do I actually volunteered to hoover the house.

Then, when Samuel had come in from his paper round and Claude had finished his GCSE coursework, I got them to help me practise taking penalties in the back garden. That lasted until Mum knocked on the window and said it was time to go.

The butterflies really kicked in then. It didn't help that Mowborough Park was rammed with people. It seemed it wasn't just girls' teams taking part but boys' too. We needed a map just to find out where we were. No prizes for guessing whose pitch was the one furthest away!

When we found it, nobody from the Belles had arrived but most of our families were milling around. All Nika's family were there, including her uncle Stan, who was painstakingly making his way across the grass with his walking frame. Lucy's mum, dad and brother Harry (who hated football) had come, as had Megan's mum, dad and auntie Mandy. They were setting up camping chairs near the goals. With them were Petra's parents and her sister Charlotte, who had brought a gang of mates. Even Amy's mum had turned up, but she spent most of her time grabbing Amy's arm and trying not to fall over in her spiky heels. There was no sign of Gemma. "She's coming. Don't worry," Amy reassured me.

"I hope so," I said. My legs were shaking. I needed her near by or the tent pegs would be back, I just knew it.

After a guy from the district league welcomed us all, we had team photos taken. It wasn't until we headed back to our pitches I realized that Gemma wasn't the only one who hadn't appeared. Nor had the Belles.

An official hurried over to Hannah. It turned out their minibus was stuck in traffic because a lorry had spilt timber over the carriageway. "Wooden you know it," I said.

Everyone groaned. "I'm nervous. It's the best I can do!" I protested.

Our opposition finally arrived at half past two, by which time all the other matches were well under way. Their coach, Layla Hodge, demanded at least another half an hour to prepare, but the official gave her ten minutes tops, so an argument broke out. While all that was going on, Lucy started yanking my arm. "How come she's stripping off?" she wanted to know. There, bang in the middle of the Belles' huge squad, was Bend it like Becky. She was shrugging out of her tracksuit top and brushing down her pristine white Belles shirt. "I thought she was with the centre of excellence?"

"Looks like she came back."

"Unbelievable," Lucy muttered. "Absolutely unbelievable."

19

We were already tense, so when word spread that Bend it like Becky was playing, it really threw us. "Thank goodness I'm not on first," Amy said. "She's like a tank!"

We started badly and were punished for it. Becky scored twice in the first five minutes and another player almost grabbed a third. Megan was fuming. "Mark up, then!" she shouted to Lucy and Holly.

That was easier said than done. I don't know how long Becky had stayed in the centre of excellence but it had honed her skills no end. She was so fast and so quick on the turn. She was hard, too, lunging in with fearsome sliding tackles to win the ball back if we dared hold possession for more than a minute.

Her team-mates tried to follow her lead, especially

the girl with the red fringe who had stopped Nika's goal last time, but her tackles were much clumsier and more dangerous. The ref pulled her up about them several times – although he resisted JJ's "advice" to send her off.

"Fall back to support, Evo," Hannah told me, making a sweeping motion with her hand.

I did as I was asked. Hannah wanted us deep, so that the scoreline didn't get worse. We began to block and were able to intercept their passes and move the ball about better, but with six of us in defence it meant we weren't creating many opportunities to score. Then, right on half-time, the Belles got a third goal with a diving header Megan had no chance of saving.

We couldn't help feeling gloomy at half-time. Megan was raging about Bend it like Becky and demanding a full enquiry. Hannah and Katie just shrugged it off. "She was dropped from the centre of excellence. She's eligible," Hannah said.

While they all argued I glanced across the field to give Mum and the bros a quick wave. My heart soared when I saw Kriss and Gemma were with them. I looked around for Amy, but she was walking towards the loos in the opposite direction. I flew across the pitch and grabbed Gemma's arm. "Come and say hello to us."

"I don't want to interfere…" Gemma began, pulling back.

"You're not interfering. This is your team. It'll give them a boost seeing you."

"I'd rather stay here."

Her eyes filled with panic but I was panicking too. "Please, Gemma. For me. I play better when you're close."

She relented then. "OK," she said.

Hannah was beginning her team talk but broke off as we approached. "Now, then, superstar," she said.

Gemma flinched. "I've only come to watch. Hope that's OK?"

"Course it is," Hannah said as everyone tried to hide the disappointment in their faces. "The rest of you just go out there and enjoy yourselves. You are awesome and that's all that matters. Right, then. Amy, you on for Eve, OK?"

"If you insist," Amy said and started stripping off.

JJ's head swivelled round but I stepped in before she had chance to say anything. Even if Amy was a girlie-girl who fainted at the sight of a free kick she was as much of a Parr as the rest of us and deserved the same respect. "Gimme some skin, girlfriend," I said loudly, high-fiving her. "Now go kick some butt."

She grinned. "OK, I'll go kick some butt."

No word of a lie, Amy scored soon after. I don't know how. I think it was an accident as the ball rebounded off her shin. Gemma and I laughed so much as JJ just stood there, mouth open. She was the first one to congratulate her, though. "Nice one, mush," she told her.

We had a stupendous spell after that. Nika and JJ were outstanding and Becky and Red Fringe were getting frustrated. "Stay on 'em, then!" their coach demanded.

They couldn't, though. Nika and JJ were linking up so well. "JJ's not retaliating at all against that girl's tackles!" I pointed out.

"That's because I've told her I'll thump her if she does." Katie laughed.

As if to reward her restraint, JJ scored with a beautiful volley from outside the box. Yes! You should have heard our spectators cheer. "How'd you like them apples?" JJ told Red Fringe as she walked back to the centre spot. Two–three. Game on!

As the whistle blew, Gemma made a heartfelt sound – something between a sigh and a groan – and I knew she wanted to play. Really, really wanted to play; as much as me, as much as JJ, as much as Megan, but when I slid my arm through hers I could feel her shaking and I knew she wasn't ready yet.

"You're being really brave," I said quietly.

"It helps having Dad here," she admitted, glancing across at him.

"Yeah," I said. "It must do."

Neither of us spoke for a while and then I was swapped in for Petra. "Stay up front this time," Hannah told me. "Tell everyone to go for it."

"Yes, coach."

I gave Gemma a quick hug, high-fived Petra and took a deep breath. This was it. The last twenty minutes of football with the Parrs. I decided I wouldn't spend it worrying or wishing things could be different. I'd just enjoy it. That was the plan anyway – until something awful happened.

Nika had been running on to the ball when Red Fringe took her legs out from behind her. She flew in the air and smacked to the ground with such force everyone winced. The girl apologized and was given a talking to by the ref, but poor Nika was in tears as she limped off. My mum and Megan's mum, being nurses, dashed over to attend to her.

"It's yours, Eve," Hannah told me.

This time I didn't miss that penalty because when I looked around for my partner she was there. I took that ball and buried it. Three–three.

Petra was called back on. Without Nika, though, we had lost some of our strength in the middle and Bend it like Becky was soon running the show again.

Not long after my equalizer they had a corner. Becky took it and everyone in the crowded goalmouth rose. I was further back, so I saw exactly what happened next. The ball was coming fast at head height. Megan jumped up to punch it out but as she did she clashed with one of their forwards. The sound of cracking skulls reverberated around the ground and we all ran across to help them.

The Belles player was crying and rubbing the back of her head. Megan was crouched, her bandana all skew-whiff, one hand on the ground to steady herself. Petra knelt beside her. "Megan, are you OK?"

Megan nodded slightly but we could tell something was wrong. She was rigid.

"Megan," Petra said again, a catch in her voice.

I bit my lip. Why wasn't she responding?

The referee was looking concerned. "Come on, pet. You'll either have to get up or leave the pitch," he coaxed.

Megan turned her head slowly, as if every movement was a struggle. She glanced up at him through pain-shot eyes. "I aren't leaving," she said, despite the rest of us gasping in shock. Her face was covered in blood: her nose was gushing bucketfuls of the stuff.

The ref waved us all back so that Hannah and Katie could get to her. "Off you come. We can't have you playing in this state. You know the rules," the ref said.

"Rules suck!" Megan declared as she unstrapped her gloves and handed them to Holly.

Everyone in the crowd began clapping as Megan left the field, but we were shaken. Megan was our talisman, our general. What would we do without her? I could see that Petra was trembling. Next to her, JJ was kicking lumps out of the pitch and Holly looked nervous as she strode towards the goal. On top of all that we were a player short. Lucy clapped her hands together. "Come on, Parrs. It isn't over yet."

"Exactly. I don't hear no fat lady singing!" I joked, trying to sound upbeat. "We can do this!"

"We can now," Amy said. "Eve, look." I turned and she nodded towards the touchline. It was like a scene from an action film. My mum was kneeling next to Nika, applying an ice pack to her ankle, Megan's mum was trying to stem the flow of blood from her daughter's nose and Gemma was pulling a Parrs shirt on. I rubbed my eyes, like they do in cartoons just to double check I wasn't seeing things, but no, it was definitely happening. Gemma was getting ready to play.

"Ready?" the ref asked as Hannah called for the swap to be made.

"Ready?" Hannah asked Gemma.

Gemma nodded. "I'm ready," she said.

You think I'm going to say that when Gemma came on something magical happened, aren't you? You think I'm going to say that, with her back on the side, we played like we'd never played before? You think I'm going to say that Gemma was beyond brilliant and made Bend it like Becky look average? You think I'm going to say that Gemma scored the winner in the last minute and we all leapt on her and nearly squashed her flat and Amy and I cried our eyes out?

Well, I'm sorry but that didn't happen.

It wasn't the last minute, it was the last but one minute. Get your facts right, dude.

Final Whistle

There's more! Despite Gemma's show-
stopping performance there was no time
to celebrate. We had injuries to our
people, people. Nika was fine — she
had a bruised and swollen ankle but
nothing too serious. Poor Megan's
nose, though, had a hairline fracture.
"Stand back, stand back," the nurse
in A&E told us as we all crowded round
to look. (And I mean all. Luckily, A&E
was quiet and Mum knew the duty staff,
so we were allowed in.)

Megan, emerging from behind the
treatment-room curtain, her nose
swollen beneath two neat strips of
dressing, beamed at us. "So who wants
to polish it first?" she asked.

The nurse frowned, thinking she
meant her nose, but of course we all
knew what she meant and you do, too.
The Nettie Honeyball Cup, of course!

Hannah handed it to her. Our brave captain lifted it above her head and we all cheered and started singing: "We're on our way to Wembley dar-da-dar-da…" And do you want to know the best bit? Gemma was singing it louder than any of us.

So that's it. The end of season two and the end of the road for me as a Parr. We did look into Lucy's idea of forming an Under 12s team but the rules change too much at that level. Under 12s play eleven-a-side on a full-sized pitch with offside and all that. Some of us could have coped with that but not all, so we decided not to try. It's not the end of the story, though. No way, dude.

There's still plenty going on.

There's the presentation evening for a start. You'd have to be crazy to miss Amy telling you about that next. Then you need to find out about Megan's plans for the Parrs' new season and what happened to me, Lucy, Gemma, Nika, Amy and Holly.

By the way, you know that saying "every picture tells a story"? Well, I figured that every fixture tells a story, too, so instead of chucking my fixture list in the bin after the final I smoothed it out and slid it into my achievements box. It reminds me that no matter how gloomy things seem at the time there's always a light at the end of the players' tunnel! To quote Mr Glasshouse: "Am I right or am I right?"

Your friend, always,
Eve xxx